the News CREW

OH, SNAP!

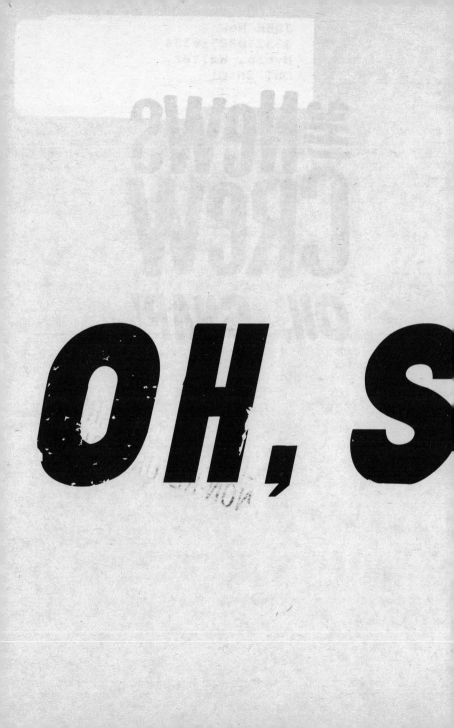

OH, S

the News Crew

SNAP!

WALTER DEAN MYERS

SCHOLASTIC INC.

Copyright © 2013 by Walter Dean Myers

This book was originally published in hardcover by Scholastic Press in 2013.

All rights reserved. Published by Scholastic Inc., *Publishers since 1920*. SCHOLASTIC and associated logos are trademarks and/or registered trademarks of Scholastic Inc.

The publisher does not have any control over and does not assume any responsibility for author or third-party websites or their content.

No part of this publication may be reproduced, stored in a retrieval system, or transmitted in any form or by any means, electronic, mechanical, photocopying, recording, or otherwise, without written permission of the publisher. For information regarding permission, write to Scholastic Inc., Attention: Permissions Department, 557 Broadway, New York, NY 10012.

This book is a work of fiction. Names, characters, places, and incidents are either the product of the author's imagination or are used fictitiously, and any resemblance to actual persons, living or dead, business establishments, events, or locales is entirely coincidental.

ISBN 978-0-545-82877-2

10 9 8 7 6 5 4 3 2 1   15 16 17 18 19

Printed in the U.S.A. 40
First printing 2015
Originally published as *The Cruisers: Oh, Snap!*

The text type was set in Adobe Caslon Pro.
The display type was set in Goshen and Nova.
Book design by Elizabeth Parisi and Carol Ly

To Jackie O'Brien

CHAPTER ONE

O, How the Innocent Must Suffer!

So there I am, sitting in Mr. Culpepper's office being my natural self, which is pretty cool, and there is Ashley Schmidt like she's ready to punch out the world, starting with me.

"So what exactly is your complaint, Miss Schmidt?"

"My complaint," said Ashley, shooting another glance in my direction, "is that the School Journalism Association has just put out its list of best school newspapers. The *Spectator* is published at Stuyvesant and that came out in first place."

"Stuyvesant is a respectable high school." Mr. Culpepper's voice sounded tired. "And the Da Vinci Academy for the Gifted and Talented is a middle school."

"*The Verdict*, published at Cardozo, came in second." Ashley's fists were balled up.

"Yes, another high-school paper." Mr. Culpepper glanced over at me.

"And *The Cruiser* came in third!" Ashley shot a mean look in my direction. "That poor excuse for journalism is not even the official Da Vinci newspaper!"

"And the School Journalism Association has no official standing, either," Mr. Culpepper said. "So whatever they said or however they ranked the newspapers makes no difference."

"It makes a difference to me!" Ashley protested. "I didn't even know they were ranking the papers, but some-one — someone must have sent them copies of *The Cruiser* without even letting me or the school know. And I think that *someone* was Alexander Scott!"

"Mr. Scott?" Our assistant principal raised one eyebrow as he glared at me.

"Some kids from Frederick Douglass Academy asked me for some back copies of *The Cruiser*," I said. "I didn't know what they were going to do with them. Ashley is just mad because *The Cruiser* is a better paper than *The Palette*. I mean, everybody knows that."

"I wouldn't go that — Ashley, do not cry in my office." Mr. Culpepper rolled his eyes upward. "Look, I think you're making a rather inflated deal over nothing. Why not look at this as a challenge to *The Palette*?"

"Yes, sir." Ashley was talking through clenched teeth. "I will do exactly that. Did you get the letter I sent you?"

"Yes, and I think it's a brilliant idea to reprint two hundred words from the British newspaper the *Guardian* each month," Mr. Culpepper said, handing Ashley a tissue. "I used to read the *Guardian* on a regular basis when I worked in London. And now that you have their official permission to reprint from their editorial pages it should add significantly to Da Vinci's official paper."

Ashley stood and gave me another mean look. She didn't say anything in front of Mr. Culpepper, but outside of the assistant principal's office she made herself pretty clear.

"I'm going to bury you and your stupid newspaper!" she hissed at me before starting down the hall.

In a way I could see her point. As the editor of *The Palette* she had a lot of pride in the paper. She also worked hard to keep up its standards. But, hey, it wasn't my fault if *The Cruiser* got third citywide.

I called a meeting of the Cruisers for 11:15 in the media center. When we got there I saw the staff of *The Palette* already in one corner, so we took the corner nearest the window.

"Why are they giving us dirty looks?" LaShonda asked.

"Because of us being picked as third-best newspaper," I said.

"They don't know that it doesn't mean anything?" Kambui asked.

"Ashley is hurt because they picked *The Cruiser* over her paper," I said. "She would have been fine if they had picked another high-school paper or even a middle-school paper, but she's embarrassed that they picked us."

"So let's just tell them to forget about it." Bobbi McCall was being cool, as per usual. "Ashley's good people."

"She's good, but she said that *The Palette* is going to bury us," I said. "And that sucks."

"Yo, dueling editorials," Kambui said. "That's kind of all right. I like it."

"Yo, Zander, check this out." LaShonda put her hands palms down on the media center table. "We're the Cruisers because we don't get into that competition thing. If Ashley wants to get all worked up over it, let her go for it."

"Okay, but she's got permission to reprint material from the *Guardian*, an English newspaper," I said.

"So?" Bobbi.

"So that's going to make *The Palette* look really classy, just when everybody is paying more attention to our paper," I said. "We're, like, the voice of the people, and Ashley's paper is, like, what?"

"The real deal," Kambui said. "They're the official school paper, and we're, like, the underground rag."

"I thought that's what we wanted to be," Bobbi said.

"Underground, but not *buried* underground," I said. "What makes us a good newspaper — and what got us the number three rating — is that we speak the truth out loud when *The Palette* is sort of edging around it."

"So what do you want to do?" LaShonda asked. "Go beat them up?"

"No, let's find a way of upgrading our paper, too," I said. "Maybe we can hook up some guest editorials."

"We could run more photos," Kambui said.

That was a good idea and I should have known that Kambui was going to come up with it because photography is his thing. LaShonda said she would do some thinking about getting the paper together, but Bobbi wasn't too hot for the idea.

"You guys are getting into a boy thing," Bobbi said. "Lighten up!"

When our meeting was over I went to lunch and the other Cruisers had classes. In the lunchroom I picked up a ham-and-cheese panini and iced tea and thought about our meeting.

Bobbi McCall was right, in a way, and we all knew it. The Cruisers had been formed when Mr. Culpepper called the four of us down to his office and complained about our grades. He ran down the whole bit about Da Vinci being a school for the gifted and talented and we were just scraping by. When he pointed out that none of us were involved in extracurricular activities we formed a club and called it the Cruisers. We also started a newspaper, and Ashley, who was editor of the official school newspaper, *The Palette*, had always been our biggest supporter. Nobody wanted to fight her or the school newspaper. On the other hand, she had a lot of pride in the paper and had been hurt when our paper was mentioned and hers wasn't. Like Bobbi, I didn't want to fight Ashley, but I didn't think I had to lie down and die just because she was upset.

The rest of the day went by slowly, with the biggest thing that happened being a puppy got into the school and everybody was chasing it around the hallway. The puppy thought we were playing but Mr. Culpepper got uptight and said he was calling the SPCA. Then Cody, the fastest kid in the school, caught the dog and gave it to Mrs. Maxwell, our principal. She carried the puppy around for a while and then gave it to the security guard, who took it outside.

"That's your kind of story, isn't it?" Ashley said when she saw me in the hallway. "You know — dog runs around in hallway as gifted and talented kids give chase?"

Ouch!

CHAPTER TWO

The Best Laid Plans of Mice and Men, Gang Aft Agley

Okay, so Ashley was getting me a little mad. Not mad big-time, but a little mad. I tried to put it out of my mind by the time I got home but I did tell Mom, who was soaking her feet in smelly water.

"Why are you doing that?" I asked. "You going for a stinky feet commercial?"

"It's plain water and white vinegar," Mom said. She was flipping through the channels with the remote, sound off, the way she always does. "It kills fungus on your feet if you have any."

"You got fungus on your feet?"

"Nope, but if I did have, the white vinegar would kill it," Mom said. "So what are you going to do about your newspaper?"

"Nothing much," I said. "No use in starting a fight with Ashley."

"One time I had a good friend named Marlene Clark," Mom went on. "We were really close until she started talking about me getting a hands commercial that she wanted. I didn't think much of it but she kept it up. Then, the next thing I knew, her agency was talking about how the two of us were competing for jobs. The next thing I knew, she was getting some of the jobs I had been getting. She used the her-against-me thing to jump right over me."

"You think that's what Ashley's doing?"

"She might not be thinking like that," Mom said. "But she sees that your paper is doing well and she might just be a little bit green-eyed."

"She's got gray eyes," I said.

"Jealous. If you're green-eyed it means you're jealous," Mom said.

"What are we having for dinner?" I asked. "You buy anything?"

"Spaghetti and meatballs. I made the sauce myself, too."

I went to the kitchen to see if she really had made the

sauce and saw the pot on the back burner over a low light. I took a spoonful of the sauce and it wasn't bad.

Mom is a model, so I could see other models competing with her for the same job. The whole modeling world is a little crazy. Sometimes agencies will call her and ask if she'd do a bumblebee, or look sexy standing near a car. Once she had to fly all the way to Chicago and stand next to a car with a leopard on a leash, and then they didn't use the photos they took because Mom was too tall. They wanted somebody tall and elegant, but not too tall because the car was small, and not too elegant because the big feature on the car was gas mileage, not looks.

"I think that there's always going to be room for two papers at Da Vinci," I said when I went back into the living room.

"Could be," Mom said.

"What's that mean?"

"Just 'could be,'" Mom said.

I looked over my homework assignments, saw that I had an essay due in two days, and thought I'd watch some television as I outlined it. Mom had bought an exercise band and was doing a routine in the living room, so I settled in my bedroom and was trying to work the remote with my toes (which I'm pretty good at) when Kambui called.

"How about I take photographs of kids in the school, and then we run them with funny captions?" he said. "Like, 'what is he *thinking*?'"

"Culpepper might not like that," I said. "How about taking photos around the city? That way you get more variety."

"Good idea," Kambui answered. "I'll get on it. Oh, by the way, did you get the tweet from *The Palette*? It's from Ashley," Kambui said. "She's asking the student body to send in their definition of a real newspaper. And Zhade Hopkins said that there's kind of a nasty editorial in *The Palette*, too."

"You smell trouble?" I asked.

"I do be smelling it," Kambui said.

THE PALETTE

A Modest Proposal

By Ashley Schmidt

It strikes me as both sad and melancholy when reading the various newspapers of the modern world to see how many bad stories are competing for attention. They parade themselves as celebrity happenings, as when an intoxicated young woman falls out of a hotel window. Sometimes they pretend to be of public interest, as when some hunk wannabe "discovers" a new cure for his addiction. The problem with all of these stories is that they all feel they must have some connection with the truth. I suggest that we cut this precious cord and let the pretend newspapers take their rightful pose as light entertainment. That way, their staffs can Cruise freely through the editorial process unhampered by a need to make more of their "reporting" than mere typing exercises.

THE CRUISER

C IS FOR ???

By Zander Scott

Apparently *The Palette* is celebrating the letter *C* in its editorials by capitalizing that letter in the word "Cruise." Other *C* words they could have used were "catty," "callow," and "caustic." The editorial board thought it had another word but, alas, there is no *C* in *sour grapes*.

CHAPTER THREE

Ghetto à la Mode

You can't sell ten dresses at a time in a big mall like this," I said. Me, LaShonda, and Kambui had just gotten out of the rain and into the Olde Harlem Mall. "And you especially can't sell to the Gap. They only buy, like, a million dresses at a time."

"I think maybe I can," LaShonda said. "Anyway, it's worth a try. Are you afraid of trying?"

"No, but I don't want to look stupid, either," I said.

"You guys go on," Kambui said. "I'm going to go around the mall and take some photos."

LaShonda and I went into the Gap and she took my arm, which meant that she wasn't as confident as she said she was. But LaShonda is good people and when she calls me sometimes to watch her back I'm glad to do it. What I thought was going to happen was that the people at the Gap were just going to look at us as middle-school kids (which we were) and young (ditto) and smile at us as they said no. But, as my mom always says, if you aren't asking some dude to spare your life, "no" isn't really that terrible.

LaShonda started looking around at some of the denim dresses, pulling me along, and before too long a guy with muscles in his forehead came over to us and asked if he could help.

"We're looking for the special markets manager," LaShonda said.

Muscle Head looked us up and down and then grunted something that might have been "What you want to see him for?" Or it might just have been indigestion.

"We have a business proposal, of course!" LaShonda was getting her confidence back.

Muscle Head gave us a hard look but produced his radio and called somebody. Then he told us to wait a minute and stretched his neck as he started looking around. He had muscles on his Adam's apple, too.

Shortly a skinny little white woman with a smile bigger than she was came over to us.

"And how can I help you guys?" she asked.

"We represent You-Nique Fashions," LaShonda said. "What we would love to do is to have you carry our line of You-Nique fashions, just ten pieces per month, in the Gap."

"Oh, well, we only deal in gross lots," Miss Big Smile said, turning her head to one side and tilting the smile. "A gross is a hundred forty-four pieces, a lot more than ten. But thank you ever so much for dropping in."

"Our marketing idea is that ten, and only ten, lucky customers get the chance to buy something unique that no other customers will have," LaShonda said. "And we are neighborhood people."

"You might have read about LaShonda's designs for the stage in the *New York Times*," I added, being pretty smart.

Miss Big Smile's smile changed slightly and she turned her head just a little bit away as she looked us up and down.

"You go to that school on One Hundred Forty-First Street?"

"Da Vinci," I said.

"And do you have your proposal written up?"

"Not yet, but —"

"Yes!" LaShonda said, swinging her backpack off her shoulder. She whipped out a small presentation notebook and handed it to Miss Big Smile.

Miss Big Smile opened the presentation case, turned quickly to the last page, checked something, and then turned to the first page. I could see there were drawings in the book and felt stupid for having started to say that we didn't have a write-up.

"You know, this is different," Miss Big Smile said finally.

"We thought you would appreciate that," LaShonda said.

"My name is Ellen Carter, and I do work with some of the buyers here. You know what I'll do, I'll talk to some people in special sales," the woman said, closing LaShonda's presentation case. "They'll talk it over and give you a call within three weeks or so. Fair enough?"

"Fair enough!" LaShonda said. "May I have your card?"

I had a million questions for LaShonda and couldn't wait to get out of the store. Besides feeling really glad for my homegirl I also felt a little like I was the only one back there who didn't know where the happenings were.

We stopped for smoothies and LaShonda laid her whole plan on me.

"I've put together a group of women in the neighborhood who sew. Most of them are either stay-at-home moms or unemployed. Every month we can come up with ten You-Nique designs for either shirts or two-piece numbers," she said. "Then the store puts them in one corner and announces that they are for sale and they won't be duplicated. We tailor the piece to whoever buys it."

"How are you making money?" I asked.

"Whoever's piece is sold gets paid for it and the tailoring," LaShonda said. "Then, maybe, if things go right, one day I'll be able to open my own design house. What do you think?"

"Sounds good to me."

"And the Gap gets all kinds of publicity because it's a community project. They make a few dollars on the item, they get people coming into the store to see what they can buy that's You-Nique, and everybody is happy."

"I wish I had thought of that idea," I said.

"How are you going to think that deep when you're only a guy?" LaShonda asked. "I mean, it's nothing personal, but you are a guy, right?"

That was seriously stupid, but I liked it.

Kambui found us just as we were finishing our smoothies, and he had somebody with him. Caren Culpepper.

"Yo, Caren, what you doing, slumming?"

"They go for it, LaShonda?" Caren asked, ignoring me.

"Yes, they did," LaShonda said. "They said they would get back to me in a couple of weeks. I think she'll either go for it or come back with a counteroffer."

"If nothing else, she's looking at your designs," Caren said.

"If Caren knew about it, why didn't you take her along?" I asked.

"Because I needed a big, strong mansy-wansy to hold on to," LaShonda cooed at me.

"Yo, I feel used," I said.

"Zander, take a chill pill!" LaShonda said. "You supported me when I needed support, the way you always do, the way the Cruisers always do. I believe in this project, but I know it didn't have to go right and I wasn't all that confident. Thanks for being there for me."

"Hey, man, Caren's got another project going," Kambui said, grinning.

I looked over at LaShonda and she was grinning, too.

"What project?" I asked.

"Caren's going to be the new press agent for the Cruisers," LaShonda answered.

THE CRUISER

The Cruiser thanks all of the students who submitted poetry for the Post–Valentine Day poetry slam. We're sorry no one tried a villanelle, but the poems were fun to read.

FROM SHANTESE HOPKINS TO YOU KNOW WHO

There is a young man in History

He makes me all Facebook and Twittery

I'd love him sooo much

(You know — kissing and stuff!)

If he paid more attention to me

FROM DEMETRIUS BROWN TO RAMONA MALDONALDO

A certain Latina from 135th

Is absolutely my favorite Mith!

She has beauty and tact

And I know for a fact

She's the chica I'd most like to kith!

FROM MICHAEL WILLIAMS TO KAREN

My mouth goes dry, my eyes go squinchy

When I see you in Da Vinci

I'm not that handsome,

Don't have a king's ransom.

FROM CONNIE TO JOHN BRENDEL

How do you conjugate a verb

To a guy who's so superb?

I was **amo-ing,** **amas-*sing,*** *and* **amat-*in'***

When I rapped to him in Latin

But he clicked his heels and started squirming

As he rapped to me in German

I said "whoa" and

"Let's just keep this set in Czech"

CHAPTER FOUR
All the World's a Stage, Kinda

Okay, so some days are okay and some days are going to be disasters, and if you pay attention, you can figure them out early in the morning.

"So there I am with Cheerios, English muffins, eggs, and broccoli, and Mom crying," I said to Bobbi McCall as we sat in the library. "This was breakfast."

"You ask her why she was crying?" Bobbi was working on her computer as we talked.

"Of course I did," I answered. "And she just kept boohooing away and said that life wasn't fair."

"Zander, what's the bottom line to this story?" Bobbi looked up.

"My dad got a part in a movie," I said. "He left a message on the phone. The dude didn't even have the decency to talk to her in person."

"Okay, so she's so happy for him that she's crying tears of joy?"

"No, she's so pissed that he got a part in a movie and she's never had a part in a movie even though she's a model and an actress," I said.

"So how did the Cheerios and English muffins and broccoli come in?"

"The news of my father getting into a movie got her confused," I said. "Whenever something good happens to him she gets upset like this."

"I gotta get to Math," Bobbi said. "I'm presenting a problem for the class to solve."

"Which is?"

"If in a straight line, ACB, AC over AB is equal to CB over AC, then we get the divine proportion, right?"

"We do?" I asked.

"And since we find this throughout nature and in the Fibonacci series, there must be something spooky about it, right?" Bobbi leaned forward and squinched up at me.

"Go on."

"Then the problem is whether or not there is a philosophical equivalent that explains human life," she said, shutting down her computer.

"That doesn't make any sense," I said. "Part of your problem is math and you're looking for an answer in philosophy. That doesn't fit my universe."

"Yeah, ain't that cool?" Bobbi stuffed her gear into her backpack and headed off.

Some things you need to leave alone. Bobbi's *math* problem was one of them.

What I had hoped was that she would have told me something cool to say to Mom. I had thought about calling my father, who's a weatherman in Portland, and telling him that it wasn't right of him to diss Mom like that.

"Yo, Dad, it's not right for you to get the break that Mom wanted, and if you did luck up and get it you should at least call and apologize."

I guess the thing was that if you were married you should stay married because if you didn't stay married then you had to worry all the time about how your ex-husband or ex-wife was doing. At least that was the way it was with my folks. Dad was a weatherman with a new wife out in Seattle, and Mom was a model in New York. She wanted a career in show business and what he wanted most was a tsunami to report. Tsunamis always ran at the top of the news. He also had a different wife (Caroline) and a daughter; and we had a little truce going. They didn't push the sister bit and I didn't send any drones their way. Seattle had enough bad weather to satisfy the dude, and at least his new family didn't bother me. But him getting a role in a movie was foul, and Mom was hurt. I could see that.

So I'm trying to figure out how to get Mom out of her blue funk and halfway trying to figure out what Bobbi was talking about with her math problem, so I don't even notice that all of the kids on the third floor are standing against the wall.

"Mr. Scott! Stand against the wall!" I hear Mr. Siegfried's voice and I look around and I see everybody with their backs to the wall and their books at their feet.

"It's a police raid!" This from Cody Weinstein.

And sure enough, that's exactly what it was about. A small army of cops was in the school looking for somebody. And they found him, handcuffed him, and took him out of the school.

Anthony Williams, aka Phat Tony, was one of the Genius Gangstas. They went around acting tough, wearing their pants low and their sneakers untied (unless Mr.

Culpepper was around). But they all got good grades so nobody could really mess with them. When the police took Tony out, all of Da Vinci Academy was buzzing.

The rumors were flying off the walls. Somebody said that Phat Tony had brought an UZI to school, and two fifth-graders said he was part of a terrorist group. I knew Phat Tony lived downtown on 84th Street and was a make-believe hoodlum so I didn't go for any of the stories. Anyway, I had my own problems to deal with.

Sometimes, one problem in your life can give you a clue for how to handle other problems. At breakfast, when Mom was crying over Dad's getting a movie role, I thought it was pretty stupid. I mean, what was I going to say? Maybe he'll get hit by a car on the way to the film studio? Mom would really be upset by that, especially if it happened when she was putting her pouty mojo on him, which was what she was doing.

Mom's pouty mojo was how she looked when she was really mad at you and hoped something bad would happen to you but she didn't want to say that something bad should happen to you because she wasn't that kind of person *BUT* if something bad did happen to you she wouldn't mind.

So I didn't know what to say to Mom to make things better and I had just put her and Ashley in the same pot because I knew Ashley was having problems with *The Cruiser* because it had come in third citywide and she thought *The Palette* was a better paper. So what I did, in my head, was to think it was a girl thing they had going on. Until I got to Math.

"So the homework is simple," Mr. Manley said. "There's a line, ACB. AC over AB is equal to CB over AC. Find out why that's significant and find as many instances as you can when the ratio of these proportions is found in nature. I want your answer and also what you think of the implications."

THE CRUISER

AN ODE TO FIBONACCI

By Bobbi McCall

I

Sometimes

Need to be

Away from Gifted

Secure in my own closed closet

Where nothing is expected except I take my turn

At being what has been ordained

Perhaps girl, or not

Or Stranger

Never

Me

CHAPTER FIVE

Tings Ain't Vat Dey Seam 2B

"So let me get this straight," Bobbi said. "You were just taking random shots and you saw Phat Tony and snapped a picture without saying anything to him?"

"Because every time he sees a camera he starts mugging and putting on his gangster poses," Kambui said. "I was just looking for casual shots."

"Right, and now you have a casual shot of Phat Tony with those three dudes they arrested for sticking up the jewelry store in the mall," LaShonda said. "The papers said that they had leads but nothing definite. Isn't that what we read, Zander?"

"I think that's what I got," Kambui said. "I'm not sure."

"Yes, and we don't know that Phat Tony was even involved," I said. "And he's pleading innocent, anyway. He said he wasn't even at the mall that night."

"So what do we do?" Bobbi asked. "We keep the photograph to ourselves and let them get away with a crime?"

"Or do we turn the photograph over to the police and get them *and* Phat Tony convicted?" I asked.

"We don't know that Phat Tony was the guy with them," Kambui insisted.

"What we know, Kambui, is that something bad happened at the mall, and that we might have the key to it," I said. "Now we have to figure out what our responsibility is and to whom. Do you feel right just doing nothing?"

"We need to be thinking about Phat Tony," LaShonda said. "They're accusing him of armed robbery!"

"Armed robbery?"

"Zander, while we were at the mall trying to sell my designs some guys in hoodies were robbing the theater on the third floor," LaShonda said. "They surprised the manager and another employee, taped them up in their office, and took the money. Somebody tipped the police that it was kids from Da Vinci."

"Phat Tony had a gun?" Kambui asked.

"I don't know how they got to Phat Tony, but I know they were talking to Mr. Culpepper," LaShonda said.

"Maybe they described the guys and Mr. Culpepper recognized Phat Tony from the description."

"You said guys with hoodies," I reminded her. "That could be anybody. And how can you describe somebody and then just arrest them? You need a warrant and stuff like that. And you can't just arrest a kid, anyway. You need to have his parents around or something."

"Did he confess?" Kambui asked.

"Miss LoBretto said that Mrs. Maxwell said that Caren Culpepper told her that Mr. Culpepper said that Phat Tony said he wasn't even in the mall that night and that he was home playing video games."

"Then he's innocent," I said.

"That's not what the police are saying," LaShonda said. "They say he fits the description: a black guy wearing a hoodie and looking mean."

"It never happened," I said. "I just don't see Phat Tony being that stupid. He can act pretty stupid at times, but he's not really that dumb."

I could tell that LaShonda was worried. She wasn't into Phat Tony that much but she worried about people a lot. Just from what I heard it didn't sound like much to worry about.

I didn't think about Phat Tony or much of anything else for the rest of the day. Sometimes I like to give my brain a day off, just to show it how much I appreciate all its hard work. And because I wasn't going to push it anymore I called Bobbi McCall and asked her to give me the dope on the math problem.

"Zander, you're supposed to figure it out," Bobbi said. "You're not supposed to call me and ask for the answer."

"I thought we were tight?"

"We are," Bobbi said. "But I still need you to figure out the problem."

"Bobbi, I think you are a little weird."

"Oh, thanks, Zander, I hoped you noticed."

Mom got home late and she was still in a funk about Dad.

"I bought him a card," she said, pointing to it lying on the kitchen table.

Congratulations, it said. Nothing else. I really felt sorry for Mom.

THE CRUISER

WHAT WE ARE NOT — A LIST POEM

By LaShonda Powell

We are not threats because we wear hoodies!

We are teenagers

We are not looking to rob you because we wear

   sneakers!

We are teenagers

We are not empty-headed because we text

We are teenagers

We are not a gang because we walk together

We are teenagers

We are not dangerous because we are young

We are teenagers

CHAPTER SIX

Don't You Hate It When Your Best, Best Friend Does
Really, Really Well and You *Still* Gotta Smile?

Morning, and I was back to thinking about Ashley. Bobbi and LaShonda didn't want to get into a fight with her, and I didn't want to, either. But I liked the idea of *The Cruiser* being the best paper. Maybe it was a guy thing. Nothing wrong with that.

Mom looked normal at breakfast. She had cucumber slices under her eyes, which made her look like an alien.

"Cute cukes," I said.

"I'm thinking of painting the kitchen," she answered.

"Why are you painting the kitchen when you don't care what it looks like?" I asked.

"Maybe I should pay more attention to what it looks like," she answered. "It's all I'll ever be good for."

"What happened now?"

"Nothing, and that's the point!" She was whining as she

talked. "I'm in my thirties and nothing really big has ever happened to me."

"You had that moisturizer commercial," I said. "You said that was a breakthrough."

"It was a tiny breakthrough," she said, pulling her legs up under her in the lotus position. "But I'm still just getting spots on ads, and no one wants me for even a small role with any real meat in it. I can do drama, I can do comedy, and I can sing. So what do they offer me?"

She hopped down from the stool she was sitting on and got a bottle of dishwashing liquid from the counter. Then she held it across her body at just the right angle so you could see the whole label and started a made-up spiel.

"*Try Free and Clean! Its sudsy bubbles will have you out of the kitchen before you know it!* Now, isn't that exciting?"

"If they run it a bunch of times and you make a lot of money from it, then it's exciting," I said.

"Zander, you don't even care if I get a break," she said, shoulders sagging. "You don't even care! How good is a dishwashing ad?"

"How about that actress who got the job selling insurance?" I asked. "She was almost forty when she got that gig."

Mom threw the bottle of dishwashing liquid into the sink and then stormed into the bathroom and slammed the door. Crap.

Half the time Mom was complaining about not making enough money. Then she complained about not getting a big role, or a magazine cover, and anytime that Dad did anything good she really suffered.

She was kind of right. She was thirty-four and nothing great was happening to her and probably nothing great was going to happen to her. Sometimes she would come home from an audition or a screen test and complain that the new girls were getting younger and younger. But that was the business she was in. She had explained to me before that being beautiful was mostly about having good bones in your face and being young. Everything else they could do with makeup.

When Mom got down about her job I knew that being calm and cool about it never helped, but I didn't think anything would help. If she had money we could go out for dinner and she could pretend that nothing bothered her. At times I thought she could have gotten married again but there was no way I was going to bring that up.

After a while she came out of the bathroom and sat

back down at the table. The cukes were gone and she had put on her foundation. Living with a model you learn about things like foundation, and bases, and all the different shades.

"You think I'm getting old and cranky?" she asked.

"Shall I say yes or no?"

"Say no."

"No."

Silence.

"How is your life going?" she asked.

"Pretty much okay," I said. "Kambui thinks he's got a picture that might get one of the kids in the school in trouble with the law but he doesn't want to give it to the police."

"Just let the kid know there's a picture around and maybe he'll go to the police himself," Mom said.

"The police already have him," I said. "They picked him up in school but he's saying that he wasn't anywhere near the place."

"Drop him an anonymous note that you know he was there," Mom said. "Then maybe he'll work out something with the police on his own."

That was some good thinking. Sneaky, but good.

So I can't wait to get to school to tell Kambui about Mom's plan. But first I have to make sure that he had the goods on Phat Tony.

"Yo, Kambui, are you sure you saw —?"

Kambui stopped me by putting a hand up and then swung his netbook out and hit a few keys. In a moment a picture of Phat Tony and three other guys that could have been his Da Vinci crew appeared. They weren't looking directly at the camera and I knew that Kambui had snapped the picture on the go.

"So what you think?" Kambui asked.

"That's definitely the Genius G man," I said.

"You think I should drop a dime on him?"

"Let me ask you. Do you think that the gun they had was real?"

"The store manager they robbed thought it was real," Kambui said. "But they wouldn't shoot me if I ratted them out, right?"

"Not more than two or three times," I said. "But maybe they'll confess and you won't have to rat them out."

"Or maybe they'll rob somebody else and shoot them," Kambui said.

"My mom has an idea."

"You told your mom?"

"She said to drop Phat Tony a note at the jail but don't sign it."

"Like in that movie." Kambui was getting excited. "I know what you did last summer. Something like that."

"Yeah."

"Except he's not in jail anymore. He's back in school. They let him out," Kambui said. "Take a look down the hall."

I turned around and saw Phat Tony and two of the other Genius Gangstas bopping down the hall. There were a zillion kids around them, and I figured Phat Tony was talking up how he had gone to jail and stuff. Weird.

What bothered me was that I had wished the whole thing with Phat Tony would just go away, and now it looked as if it might. But if he and his crew were really gangsters and ended up hurting somebody, then it was going to be on Kambui, who took the picture, and me, because I knew about it, too.

I wished he hadn't told me.

CHAPTER SEVEN
We Travel the High Seas All the Way to Merry England

Sometimes I am smart and sometimes I am soooo smart it's scary. Not weird smart like Bobbi with math or LaShonda with design, but smart enough to impress me, and that's not easy.

"So what's this brilliant idea?" LaShonda asked.

"Ashley is going to get articles from the *Guardian* in England and thinks everybody is going to fall out, right?"

"That's pretty impressive to me," Bobbi said.

"Okay, so how about we hook up with a school in London and have them contribute articles to *The Cruiser*?" I said. "I looked up a bunch of schools in and around London. One of them is Dulwich, where an Arctic explorer went. Another is Eton, whose big thing is that it's always in crossword puzzles. But then I found Phoenix, which is in London. And when I saw the pictures of their students I got hooked right away. It's, like, Diversity Digs."

I flipped on the computer monitor and then called up the Phoenix website. It was really a good-looking site and the kids who went there looked a lot like the kids at Da Vinci.

"You e-mail them?" LaShonda asked.

"Yeah, and I sent them some digital copies of *The Cruiser* and asked them if we could have a Skype date," I said. "They came back with a probable yes but they had to clear it with their school."

Bobbi and LaShonda spent the next several minutes going over the Phoenix school website. It looked great and all the Cruisers were interested.

"This is going to send Ashley up the wall," Kambui said.

"It's a gifted and talented wall," Bobbi said in a voice so soft I could hardly hear her.

"Do we have to clear it with Mrs. Maxwell?" LaShonda asked.

We all agreed that we should, and I wanted to run it by Ashley, too. I have a lot of respect for the editor of *The Palette* and she had a lot of respect for the Cruisers before the competition thing came around. I sent her an IM asking to meet with her, and she came back with a message saying a meeting would be cool.

Meanwhile, Phat Tony was running his mouth like he was campaigning for president or something. He was in school and every lunch period he was sitting with his crew talking about how the police had questioned him. Me and LaShonda wandered over to where he was holding court.

"They had me in this little room with a television camera in the corner." Phat Tony was talking with a tuna salad sandwich in one hand. "They thought I didn't notice the camera, but I was steady checking it out. I knew that everything I said could be used against me in a court of law."

"They try the good cop, bad cop trick on you?" a freshman asked. I could tell the kid was a freshman because he wore his DV Academy medallion and only freshman wore those.

"They tried everything," Phat Tony said. "They even had my mom on their side, saying how she had always told me to tell the truth."

"So where's the case now?" I asked.

"They had to let me go because they don't have any evidence," Phat Tony said. "They actually thought they had trapped François Villon in their *petite trappe*. But it don't hardly go that way, *mes amis*. They got to come down longer and harder before they get the kid."

"They take your DNA?" the freshman asked.

"They wanted to," Phat Tony said. "But I asked them if they had a search warrant. They didn't, so I told them to cop a walk!"

"They got any evidence at all?" LaShonda asked.

"They said they got a little something, but they wouldn't tell me." Phat Tony was looking smug. "This one detective kept covering up his notes so I couldn't see them. Maybe he wants me to beg him to take a peek. Maybe, instead, I'll just make him an offer he can't refuse!"

"Did you do it?" another kid asked.

"If I answered that question I'd have to kill you," Phat Tony said, looking at the kid with one eye half closed. "And that would probably ruin your whole day, wouldn't it?"

When LaShonda and I split the lunchroom I asked her if she thought Phat Tony had stuck up the store in the mall. Her "no" was really strong.

"He's talking too much," she said. "And that line about making an offer that somebody can't refuse is right from *The Godfather*."

To my mind the idea that Phat Tony was quoting from *The Godfather* didn't make him innocent. He could have been a guilty dude who happened to see a lot of movies.

THE CRUISER

THE BALLAD OF THE DEAD RAPPERS

By Phat Tony

Big L's fallen, Grym Reaper's history,

Tupac's death is a mystery

For Old Dirty Bastard we shed a tear

Oh, where are the rappers of yesteryear?

Big Pun had heart, but it gave way

Buffy from the Fat Boys has seen his last day

Biggie caught some bullets, that's what I hear

Oh, where are the rappers of yesteryear?

CHAPTER EIGHT

Doing the Right Thing Is Not Always the Right Thing to Do

Mrs. Maxwell had started a program she called Operation Leapfrog. In the program some kids from Booker Elementary who were having trouble with their reading skills came over to Da Vinci and we helped them with their reading. Mostly girls are doing the mentoring, but Mrs. Maxwell had asked some boys to at least hang out in the media center while the mentoring was going on.

Booker was on 126th Street and St. Nicholas, down the street from the park. The kids looked a little rough and I expected our girls were going to have some trouble and it happened. Five minutes into the reading sessions we heard a big noise — it sounded just like a chair falling over or something — and then a commotion. I looked up from a magazine I was reading and saw Shirley Tolentino lying on the floor and a boy, fists clenched, standing over her.

Cody was the first one over and he pushed the boy away from Shirley. The boy, from Booker, was kind of tall and went to take a swing at Cody. Cody blocked the swing, grabbed the kid's wrist, and spun him around, pinning him to the wall.

"I'm going to beat your ass, man!" the kid was sputtering.

I pushed his head against the wall and leaned against him as some of the other Da Vinci kids helped Shirley up.

"She said I can't read!" the kid was going on. "She can't read!"

"I just asked him if he could read a sentence," Shirley said. Her face was red and puffy. "And he pushed me right out of the chair."

The kid tried to struggle a little but saw he couldn't move against me and Cody, and he let his body relax.

The kid wasn't more than nine, and was a little overweight. I looked at his face to see if he was still mad and saw him start to tear up.

"Yo, push a chair to us," I said to the small knot of Da Vinci kids gathering around.

We put the kid into the chair just as the door opened and Mrs. Maxwell and Mr. Culpepper came rushing in.

Okay, so this is what happened. The kid who pushed Shirley, Syed Nolan, was put out of the program immediately and Mrs. Maxwell asked me and Cody to go home with him.

"You don't have to go inside or anything," she said. "Just make sure he gets home safely. I'll call his school."

Syed said he could go home by himself, but me and Cody went with him, anyway.

Syed was sad on the way and kept saying that Shirley should not have said he couldn't read.

"She didn't mean anything bad," I told Syed. "She was trying to help you, man."

"I don't need any help," he said.

Syed stopped in front of a building that looked deserted. Cody asked him if he lived there, and Syed puffed up as if he was going to fight again.

"If we ask our principal to let you back in the program, will you come back?" I asked.

"No."

On the way back to school Cody asked me if I thought that Syed actually lived in that building.

"It was the pits," Cody said.

"Yeah," I said. "It was, but if he doesn't want us to try to help him, there's nothing to do but let it be."

"We could tell Mrs. Maxwell," Cody said. "She'll come up with something."

"I don't know," I said. "I don't know. You remember when we were trying to help LaShonda get over and found out that what we saw as being good wasn't that good for her because of her brother?"

"Anything has to be better than living in a dump like that," Cody said.

"How about having your family separated and living in shelters?" I asked. "That might be better for us, so we can say that we did something for that kid. But would it be better for him or his family?"

Cody half shrugged and half shook his head. He didn't know, and neither did I.

Dear Cruisers,

Thank you for your interest in our school. We are sending along an attachment explaining who we are and what we are about. Although we do admire your digital paper, we're not sure what your intentions are and feel hesitant in offering a partnership. Moreover, your Cruising *philosophy seems counter to Phoenix policy and the aims of our student population. Can you inform us of why you think we should form an alliance with you, and also how you see such an alliance? Perhaps we would have a clearer idea of exactly who you are if you told us of your present concerns and editorial policies.*

Edward Mahfouz, general editor, the Phoenix Voice

"So who do they think they are?" Bobbi asked. "Why do they need a clearer idea of *exactly who we are*? Write them back and tell them that our editorial policies depend on which way the wind is blowing!"

"Suppose they contacted us," I said, "and decided they wanted to do a hookup. Would you go for it or would you say something like 'Who are you?' or 'What's your thing?' I mean, we could be racists or something."

"You think the *Guardian* asked Ashley what *The Palette* was about?" Kambui asked.

"No, but the *Guardian* doesn't have to worry about their articles being printed," I said. "If Mrs. Maxwell saw that we were printing articles from some creepy magazine or some radical Nazi paper she'd probably be a little upset.

Let's tell them what issues we're dealing with and see what they say."

"Okay, but let's keep it light so they don't think we're sucking up!" Bobbi added.

I understood Bobbi not wanting to suck up to the British school, but I was kind of excited about it. It was a different experience and I thought it might be fun.

I asked Bobbi to write up how we got to be the Cruisers, and what that meant to us. She said she would and then I asked LaShonda to do something about the neighborhood and how we wanted to improve it.

"I bet they have a whacked-out opinion of what Harlem is all about," she said. "But I will definitely set them straight!"

I asked Kambui to write something about the Genius Gangstas. He refused.

"I think they're jive," he said. "That's not, like, putting our best foot forward, or something."

"No, but it runs down who we are in accepting people," I said. "And if they can't feel that then maybe we don't want to be part of their program."

"I hear you," Kambui said. "Why don't you do it?"

I could dig where Kambui was coming from. He was creating a distance between himself and the Genius Gangstas just in case something did pop off.

Home. Mom left a note for me to check the computer.

Look at Word under the file Movie.

I made myself a grilled cheese sandwich with relish and mayonnaise, then clicked on the file she had made. It was empty except for a link line. I clicked on that and an ad came up for a movie. The movie was called *The Debt*. It starred Eleanor Sykes and Donald Scott! It was the one my father was going to be in and the date on it was from last year.

I got the whole thing in a flash. The dude had made the movie last year but he hadn't told Mom until he found out they were actually going to air it. Foul.

And it couldn't be that good if it never made the theaters. Still, I knew it was going to mean more boo-hoos and depression and there was nothing I could do about it.

I head-switched to the English kids at Phoenix and started writing about the Genius Gangstas.

The Genius Gangstas of Da Vinci are a group of guys who are soft-core rappers and who do really well with their academics even though they appear not to try very hard. Sometimes they do things that border on bullying and so I don't really feel them in any deep way. Recently there was an armed robbery at the local mall and one of the Genius Gangstas, Phat Tony, was arrested. He claimed he wasn't there, but one of our staff members actually photographed him and his crew at the mall shortly before the robbery, which proves he lied about not being there, but I still don't think he did the robbery. Anyway, I've never seen him with a gun so we're more or less letting the matter drop as far as the robbery is concerned but The Cruiser *is considering the role of the Genius Gangstas and wondering if it's good for the school or not.*

I sent the e-mail off to London, imagining my message flying across the ocean, traveling over Buckingham Palace, and landing in the school in the evening after everyone had gone home. I was wondering how the kids at Phoenix were going to answer when Mrs. Maxwell caught up with me in the hallway.

"How are you doing, Zander?" she asked.

"Good," I said.

"I'm not so good today," our principal answered. "I have some doubts about our Leapfrog program. And thank you and Cody for helping out the other day with that little boy. He reminded me that there aren't always easy answers to our problems."

"No problem," I said.

"And I'm still concerned about Anthony Williams," she went on. "I called the police today and they weren't very forthcoming. They just kept telling me that I needn't worry. There's not a chance of that when one of my pupils might be in trouble."

"You think he did the robbery?" I asked.

"No, I'm just concerned," she said. "Just concerned."

She smiled one of her quick little smiles and then walked toward her office. My first thought was that I wished I hadn't mentioned anything about the robbery in my e-mail.

RAPPERS WANTED
MUST HAVE STREET CREDS,
SWEET DREADS,
FOR INCREDIBLE RAPPENINGS,
DREADABLE HAPPENINGS,

ROLLIN' ROUGHER THAN ROUGH
ROLLIN' TOUGHER THAN TOUGH
DONE SEEN ENOUGH STUFF
TO HANG WITH
AND BANG WITH
THE EINSTEINS WITH THE SWEET MINDS
SPITTING TRUTH LIKE SWEET VERMOUTH
STYLING PAIN LIKE OLD CHAMPAGNE
WITH THE ORIGINAL FANGSTERS
THE GENIUS GANGSTAS
IF YOU AIN'T NO PHONY
CONTACT PHAT TONY

Phat Tony was playing it to the hilt. He was looking to put together a crew of rappers and had pasted flyers all over the school bulletin boards and in the boys' bathrooms. The word was that some kids were looking to hook up with him, and I heard a few trying out their rapping skills in the hallways.

So now my head was multitasking. On one side of my brain was Phat Tony styling his gangster role and using his high IQ and good grades as a backup. And I knew I was trying to move away from thinking that maybe he really was a gangster and had done the stickup. Pushing stuff out of my mind was lame, but I was trying to do it. I was even sorry that I had run my e-mouth to the British kids.

Then I thought about Syed. I didn't know if I should have gotten myself more involved with him or not. He needed help, but I didn't want to open up something I couldn't close up. With LaShonda, when they wanted to give her a scholarship that would have separated her and her brother who has autism syndrome, we were pushing back from something good because there was something better, LaShonda and her brother staying together. With Syed I didn't know what we were pushing back from. If things were really bad and somebody tried to break up his family I didn't know what I could do.

And then there was Bobbi's poem in *The Cruiser*. We ran with the poem but we really didn't discuss it much. I wanted to ask Bobbi why she wanted to back off being gifted, if that was what the poem really meant. I hadn't mentioned anything to her because I didn't know where she was coming from.

The truth was that there seemed to be a logical way of living life, and everybody could see that, but it didn't work full-time on anybody. I started thinking about Bobbi's math problem again. Well, it wasn't really a math problem so much as it was a math/philosophy problem. And I didn't know the answer to that one, either.

I ran the equation and came up with Fibonacci, so I knew I was on the right track. Then the math outran me and the ratios sneaked between my legs and left me lost.

THE PALETTE

Selling Rags
by ASHLEY SCHMIDT

Various the papers various wants produce,
The wants of fashion, elegance, and use.
Men are as various: and, if right I scan,
Each sort of paper represents some man.

Benjamin Franklin

Apparently the staff of *The Cruiser* feels the need to have a publicist to promote its journalistic efforts. All over the school we are seeing flyers appear praising the self-labeled "alternative" paper. *The Palette* wonders what standards make a paper alternative? Is it a casual attitude? Perhaps skipping the larger issues? Or is "alternative" merely a code word to cover a multitude of sins, all of which have to do with not having a core responsibility?

A GUEST EDITORIAL FROM THE PAGES OF *THE CRUISER*

WE RECEIVED THIS E-MAIL TUESDAY

Although we in the United Kingdom admire the free-spirit attitude of our American allies, we wonder if that spirit is really free or, as it so often seems, is wedded to the Old West mentality that illuminates the popular image of the land across the Atlantic. When there are groups formed calling themselves Gangstas (sic) and they are celebrated as an integral part of an educational consortium, one wonders what the educational milieu could possibly be.

We have now had an opportunity to examine both *The Palette* and *The Cruiser*, and thank the editors of the latter for sending them along. We hesitate to endorse *The Palette* simply because it lacks distinction. As to *The Cruiser*, we simply, but quite vehemently, hesitate.

Phoenix School, London, England

CHAPTER NINE

Cogito, Ergo Sum,
but If I Cogitoed and Didn't Tell Nobody, Can I Go to Jail?

Let's get back to Phat Tony." Kambui looked worried. "What did Mrs. Maxwell say?"

"Just that she called the police, and they weren't saying very much," I said. "I think they're not completely buying his story that he wasn't in the mall."

"Somebody must have dimed him in the first place," LaShonda said. "How did the police get his name?"

"I think we should just stay out of it," Bobbi said. "I don't want anybody to get in any trouble."

"What's the deal if we have a picture of him and the police find out?" Kambui asked. "Are we, you know, tampering with evidence or something?"

"Google it!" Bobbi said.

We Googled. The question was, If a person knows about a possible felony, does he or she have to report it to the police? The answer came back in the form of an answer to someone else asking the same question: *There is no legal duty to call the police if you see a crime being committed or suspect someone of a crime. But if you help to cover up the crime you can be charged with being an accessory to the crime.*

"So Kambui is in the clear?" LaShonda asked.

No one spoke for a moment, and then we all started nodding.

"Except if the police ask Kambui if he has any pictures," Bobbi said. "Then he has to say yes or no, or refuse to answer."

"No one knows about the photos except you guys," Kambui said.

"And we're not talking," I said.

"What Phat Tony does isn't my business," Bobbi said.

"I don't believe he did anything, anyway," LaShonda said.

No one was feeling good about it. We switched the conversation to English, and then to Ashley for a while, and then the meeting broke up.

Kambui was down as he stuffed some books he wanted to borrrow into his backpack. I told him not to worry about the photos.

"Just try to forget them," I said.

"What happens if Phat Tony really is a gangster and kills a kid at Da Vinci?" Kambui asked. "I saw a special on kids that kill. They had this thirteen-year-old kid who gunned down his cousin just to see how it felt."

"You want to talk to Phat Tony?" I asked. "Tell him to keep himself cool because we got photos?"

"No."

"You scared?"

"Yes."

"Oh."

"So Ashley is going around the school talking to kids in the hall and pretending she wants to interview them to get their opinions on how a newspaper should be run," Caren said. "What she's really doing is trying to get kids to like her so they'll think her paper is the best."

"Nothing wrong with that," I said.

"I didn't say anything was wrong with it," Caren said, twisting her hair around one finger. "I just noticed what she was doing. And it's okay if I'm going to talk to some kids to see if I can influence them, right?"

"Yeah, sure," I said.

What I really meant was, "Yeah, sure, if that's what you want to do." Something like that. I mean, it didn't seem like that big a deal for Caren to talk to other kids at Da Vinci.

Caren Culpepper is, like, a mystery girl. Sometimes she's super friendly, and sometimes she walks around with her nose in the air like she just smelled something bad.

The fact that I went out with her twice doesn't mean anything, but I think she thinks that I like her a lot. I don't hate Caren, and I don't really like her, but I like her in a non-boy-and-girl kind of way. If you know what I mean, which you probably don't know what I mean because when it comes to Caren Culpepper sometimes I don't even know what I mean.

And since she's Mr. Culpepper's daughter, and he's the assistant principal of the school, you can't be too mean to her.

She's kind of smart (probably studies), but in a sneaky sort of way.

She's not ugly and not pretty, just a little ordinary unless she fixes herself up. The main thing with Caren is that you never know what she's going to do next.

THE PALETTE

Thug Life

By Ashley Schmidt

The new phenomenon in American school life is the homage being paid to what is being called Thug Life. Our understanding of this is it basically started with Tupac Shakur and glorified what he considered to be the code of the streets. Now Phat Tony (aka Tony Williams) is carrying on that tradition with his raps and his appeal to violence. But is this what we truly want at Da Vinci Academy? Aren't we capable of better than "not being snitches" and "not slinging to kids"? I think that just being at Da Vinci tells more about you than Phat Tony will ever admit.

Naturally, *The Cruiser* applauds Phat Tony and even ran his very weak attempt at poetry. Is *The Cruiser* advocating Thug Life as the epitome of our school and our ambitions? One wonders if they'll supply an answer.

THE CRUISER

TO BE A THUG

By LaShonda Powell

. . . Sparkling bright and worry free!
That's just where I want to be!
Tra-la-la-la!

The Palette is sounding more and more like some kind of new detergent rather than Da Vinci's official journal. Ashley, did you ever hear the expression "walk a mile in my shoes"? I don't think you have because your mouth is running where your feet have never been! Girlfriend, check this out. Those kids choosing Thug Life are not doing it because they find it glamorous, they're doing it because they don't have the same access to the good life you are pushing. People need to find their own values when they look in the mirror, not yours. And yes, I can see that what you are running in your bourgeois newspaper is culturally hip, and perhaps superior to many kinds of Thug Life, Street Life, and Funky Roll Lane! BUT until you can create a system in which everybody can roll out of their mama's (whoever their mama is!) and directly into the Good Life, then you need to lighten up and give people some slack. WE are not all sparkling bright and worry free, honey. And yes, *The Cruiser* is open to people who have wandered off the Golden Path. We understand that all paths are not golden, but they are all human.

CHAPTER TEN

Act One, Scene One, the Bad Guy Rides Again!

At home. Mom is all excited and has a load of food on the table. Bobbi, who I brought over for moral support, is already digging in and has crumbs all over her face.

"So you watch it yet?" I asked. Mom had called me at school to moan about Dad sending her a DVD.

"No, but I did find out it's a pilot for a series," Mom said. "Which means that if anybody likes it they'll run the darn thing. Let's sit down and watch it."

"You going to be okay?" I asked.

"No," Mom said. "Of course not."

So, if somebody is quirky, it's Bobbi McCall. Bobbi has two platforms. One is super weird and everything is about math, and the other is super weird and everything is about being calm.

"Zander, someplace in the universe, it all comes together," Bobbi said when she settled onto my couch. "Ask your mom."

I looked at Mom and she was making a face. She didn't have a clue what Bobbi was talking about. But I knew Bobbi would calm Mom down, which is why I'd asked her to come over to watch the movie my father was in with us.

"Let's get this done," Mom said, switching on the Magic Box.

I was tense as we sat through the commercials. On one hand I didn't want Mom to be too upset because my father was doing what she really wanted to do. On the other hand it was kind of sharp watching your father in a movie.

My mouth was dry and I went to the kitchen and got some ice for my soda. When I got back to the living room there was a close-up of my father looking a little too perfect and speaking his lines as if he thought they were funny.

"So you were sitting on the porch when this car rolls up?"
"Uh-huh."
"And then what happened?"

"Two guys came out of the car, which was a Ford Taurus SE. One of them started yelling something toward the house but the other one didn't say nothing. He just brought his stick up and started shooting."

"And the other one just watched?"

"You mean the cute one?"

"Whatever."

"No, he was shooting, too. He had a silver gun. It looked a little like a Glock 38 but I really think it was a Beretta 327-A. It didn't have the kick of a Glock 38."

"Can you describe the two shooters?"

"I didn't see their faces."

Close-up on Dad. He lifts one eyebrow and shakes his head like he's figured out something.

There's a stock shot of a moon rising over some brick buildings and then setting. The next scene is of a dog sniffing a fence. Then he pees on the fence.

There's a switch to a scene in police headquarters. Dad is drinking coffee and a white policeman turns to him and asks him what's going on.

"It's the code of the ghetto," Dad says. "Nobody snitches and everybody knows the guilty party. This is having a terrible impact on the community."

"*Can you blame them?*" the white guy asks. "*They have a choice of living in fear or dying heroically. I don't know what I would do.*"

Close-up of Dad.

"*I know what I would do, Dan,*" Dad says. "*And it sure wouldn't be tolerating these creeps!*"

"Oh, my God, your father's a terrible actor!" Mom said. "I feel so bad for him."

"The story's not so good, either," I said.

We watched another fifteen minutes of the movie with Mom moaning all the way through it. She was right, though. Dad was a terrible actor. Any moment I thought he was going to turn to the camera and give the weather report.

"He's kind of a nonhero type," I said.

"I don't know," Mom answered. "Nonheroes might be the new heroes. Like guys that get shot are heroes today. Getting shot wasn't that cool years ago. You know what I mean?"

"And if you actually get killed, like Tupac and Biggie," Bobbi said, "then you get to be super big-time, but I don't think there are a lot of perks to being dead."

"But suppose he gets a television series out of this?" Mom said.

The truth was that Mom didn't want to see her ex-husband do too well, but on the other hand she didn't want to see him go down too hard, either. She was somewhere in the middle.

"I don't think he's going to get a series out of this story," I said.

"He could." Mom was kind of whining. "It's about a kind of hero and people like that kind of story."

We watched some more of the story, sometimes with the sound off, and Mom was right, the story did make him seem like a hero.

The story sort of bumped along, like it wasn't sure where it wanted to end up, and then my father, the "good guy" detective, gave a block party and everybody was laughing and singing. He was dancing badly, and the neighborhood people were laughing at him, too.

"That's really the way he dances," Mom said.

I guessed how the story was going to end. Dad had made a new set of friends and then there was a mysterious phone call that solved the case. Hmmm.

Mom said I should take Bobbi home, and Bobbi said that I should go to sleep because she didn't need anybody taking her home. I went home with her, anyway, mostly because I didn't want to hear Mom go on about the movie.

"So what do you think?" Bobbi asked. "He's good-looking enough to make movies."

"It'll kill Mom," I said. "But that bit you said about who was a hero — every time a rapper gets killed or gunned down he blows up even bigger."

"You think Fifty Cent was really shot nine times?" she asked.

"Yeah, probably."

"But that doesn't make him a hero in my book," Bobbi said. "It just means that he's lucky to be alive."

"Yeah, but you remembered how many times he was shot," I said.

"Hey, Zander?" We were in front of Bobbi's house.

"Yeah?"

"Can I ask you something personal?"

"Sure," I said.

"Do you think I'm really gifted?"

"You?" I didn't believe what she was saying. "If anybody is gifted it's you. How come you're asking?"

"Just wondered what you thought," she said. "See you tomorrow."

I took the Eighth Avenue bus uptown. What was on my mind was why Bobbi was asking me if she was gifted. She had to be one of the smartest kids in the school, if not in the world, and she had to know it. For a hot second I thought maybe she was digging me, but then I remembered her poem about being in a closet by herself and wondered if she was having problems.

When the bus reached 126th Street, a block up from St. Joseph's, my cell rang. It was Bobbi.

"So what do you think?" she asked.

"I still don't think my dad's going to make it in the movies," I said.

"Not that, Zander," Bobbi said. "Didn't you check your messages?"

"No."

"Check them and call me back," Bobbi said. "It might be time to roll out the Cruise Mobile."

I checked my messages. There was only one, a message from LaShonda saying that the Gap had accepted her design, announced it in the *Amsterdam News*, and there were already pickets at the store protesting against her.

Tuesday morning.

So I went to school, calling LaShonda as I walked. She answered and I could feel the burn from three blocks away. LaShonda was burning oxygen by the carload.

"And Charles Lord had the *nerve*! The N-E-R-V-E *NERVE!* to say I was exploiting the women doing the sewing on my designs!"

"He mentioned you by name?" I asked.

"He didn't mention me by name but he said that the Gap had some black woman *fronting* for them! Does it look to you or to anybody else in the world like I need to be *fronting* for somebody? Do I? Do I?"

"Yo, LaShonda, I didn't say it," I protested. "Look, let's call up the *Amsterdam News* and give them the —"

"They're the ones that published this sorry-butt story!" LaShonda said.

"Yeah, but they're fair," I said. "We can straighten this out. This might even work in your favor if we play it right."

"I'm too mad to be playing anything!" LaShonda said.

"LaShonda —"

"Don't be wrong, Zander man," she said. "I need somebody strong backing me up."

"I got your back," I said. "You don't have to worry over this!"

"Okay, I just might need you to punch out Charles Lord," LaShonda said.

Charles Lord had appointed himself the protector of the community and whatever an "activist" is supposed to be. He's a big guy and looks like he's in pretty good shape. He's the kind of dude who sits on the sidewalk and watches people do their thing. And if anybody is doing anything worthwhile he runs and gets in front of them and then says he's leading them. What I would like to do is to get him in a fight where he can't hit back. Seriously stupid, but I liked the thought.

So I get to Da Vinci and who is on the stairs leading to the big front doors but Zhade Hopkins, looking ridiculously good.

"Hey, Zander, what's going on?"

"I'm all good," I said. "How you doing?"

"I'm all right," she said. "But, you know, Caren is a friend of mine and I hope you don't hurt her."

"Why would I hurt Caren?"

"Boys do that kind of thing," Zhade said. "She's all upset, and I told her to have some tea and try to get herself together before classes start. She's sitting in the cafeteria now. She won't talk to anybody, she just sits there crying."

"What's that got to do with me?"

"Zander, that is so foul!"

"*What* is so foul?"

"If a girl is sitting somewhere crying and all she can say when you ask her what's wrong is some boy's name — and that's all she can say because she's too upset to go on — don't tell me the boy doesn't know what's going on."

Zhade gave me a mean look and walked away.

What I wanted to do was to go find my man Kambui to see what was going on with the police, but something told me I better check out what was going down with Caren Culpepper first.

I didn't know if she was still in the cafeteria, but I went in and started looking around.

"There he is!" someone said.

They were all looking at me. I wanted to stop and start telling them that I didn't know what was going on, but then I remembered what Zhade had said. I looked around and finally saw Caren sitting by herself in the corner.

I thought she saw me, too, but she put her head down so quickly I didn't know if she had or not. Anyway, I walked over to her. There was a chair at the end of the table and I sat down on it.

"What's up?"

Nothing.

"Yo, Caren, what's up?"

Nothing.

I knew she could hear me. I moved my chair closer and asked again.

"Caren, what's going on?"

"Zander, please don't make me tell you."

"Tell me what?"

"Put your arm around me."

"No!"

Tears. Her shoulders were shaking. I leaned closer and asked her what was up.

"Put your arm around me and I'll tell you," she said.

"But I don't really want to."

It was a lose-lose situation, and I figured it was nothing.

"You got a bet with somebody that you can get me to put my arm around you?" I asked.

"It's about Kambui," she said, almost in a whisper. "But please don't make me tell you."

I looked around the room. Everybody was looking at us. I felt embarrassed and stupid. Mostly stupid. But if it was about my boy Kambui I had to find out what was going on.

I put my arm around Caren.

"Last night," she sniffed, "about eight o'clock, the police called my house. My father got the call. He was talking to the New York City Police Department. They told him that they had received information from Scotland Yard —"

"Scotland Yard?" I moved away from Caren. "Get off my back. Scotland Yard didn't give anybody any information."

"That you had told the kids in some school in London —"

"Go on."

"Put your arm around me, so people won't think it's about the police," Caren said.

"No."

"Good, because I promised I wouldn't breathe a word," she said. "And I really want to keep my word to my father."

I put my arm around her again.

"They said that Kambui had photographs of the guys who held up the mall and that the Cruisers were keeping it secret," Caren said. "You could all be accessories after the fact."

"Oh, snap!"

"But the good news is you're all juveniles, so you won't get more than two or three years. My father was upset that I overheard his conversation, which is why I promised him I wouldn't breathe a word of this." Caren put her two arms around my waist. "He said he didn't want me anywhere near you hoodlums."

THE CRUISER

THE PERFECT AS ENEMY OF THE GOOD

By Bobbi McCall

Recently we've seen a certain community "activist" try to stop projects (and progress) by claiming that he is seeking a higher ground, the search for perfection. Charles Lord has already objected to some of the special schools in the city by claiming that all students should be offered the same programs. When it is pointed out to Mr. Lord that all students won't necessarily benefit from the programs offered at the more selective schools, he continues his ranting about his quest for the perfect world in which both schools and students are always up to the task.

Mr. Lord is also very much for limiting community opportunities unless the opportunities meet his vague standards. What I would like to suggest to Mr. Lord is that ultimately he is no different than the people he claims are trying to destroy the community. They might try to stop how the neighborhood advances in a different way, but Mr. Lord is also trying to bring an end to some of the most innovative programs and opportunities available.

The perfect can often be the enemy of the good and, in the long run, may not even exist as modeled by Charles Lord.

CHAPTER ELEVEN

"Deny Thy Father and Refuse Thy Name;
Or, If Thou Wilt Not, Be But Sworn My Love and
I'll No Longer Be a Culpepper."

As difficult as it is, we are *trying* to give you misguided children the benefit of the doubt!" Mr. Culpepper's neck seemed two sizes too large for his collar and was bulging out in a red and white circle over the blue-striped shirt. "And we need you to tell us *exactly* what you know about any crimes at the mall."

"When did we lose the right to an attorney?" LaShonda asked. "Even on the TV cop shows you get the right to an attorney!"

"Young lady —"

"She's correct." Mrs. Maxwell held up a hand, palm toward Mr. Culpepper. "I don't think we want our students telling us anything that might get them into trouble later on."

"And I, for one, don't want them doing anything or

withholding any kind of information that will bring infamy to the school, Mrs. Maxwell."

"I will take full responsibility for that, Adrian." Mrs. Maxwell's voice was still calm, but she was in control. "I would like all of you to go home and discuss this entire matter with your parents or guardians. Tell them that they are free to discuss it with either me or the Board of Education's legal department if they so choose.

"But understand this. I know you are very bright young people, but any involvement with the juvenile justice system is quite serious. There is no matter that is guaranteed to be casual when the police are concerned. The school in London — Phoenix, I believe — has made a serious charge, which should be answered. Please tell your parents as much as possible and, by all means, listen to their advice. You are free to leave now."

I looked back over at Mr. Culpepper and saw that he was still steaming. And I wasn't surprised when he followed us into the hall a moment later.

"Mr. Scott," he said in a voice that sounded like a cartoon alligator getting ready to eat a cartoon rabbit, "may I have a word with you?"

"Yeah, sure," said the cartoon rabbit.

"Perhaps in my office?"

We walked down the hall to the same office that the Cruisers had been formed in. I remembered the first time we were there, with Culpepper lecturing us on how education was an adventure on the high seas of life. What I thought I knew he was going to say this time was that he was disappointed in the Cruisers and that I had better see that we got our act together.

I was wrong.

"Young man, if I ever catch you near my daughter again I will personally tear you limb from scrawny limb, eat the residue of your wretched body, and pass it through my body into the urban wasteland that will never — mind you, *NEVER*, be part of my daughter's life. Do I make myself clear?"

"Yes, sir."

The cartoon rabbit gulped as the cartoon alligator grew larger and larger.

"Now leave my office, and stay as far away from me and from Caren as your peanut brain can *MANAGE*!"

The way I figured it, the days of the Cruisers were numbered. Even if we got out of this in one piece there was too much conflict for Mrs. Maxwell to keep supporting us.

And Mr. Culpepper would be just too eager to see us bite the dust.

I texted Bobbi and we agreed to have the Cruisers meet at the Burger Joint on 145th Street. I knew we needed to think fast if we were going to keep the Cruisers intact, and we had to have a plan that defused the situation. Something both calm and intelligent.

"Let's kidnap Phat Tony and torture him!" LaShonda said. "Make him tell us what he knows, and then, if it doesn't sound right, kill him!"

"Okay, so we've got two votes in favor of torturing Phat Tony," Bobbi said. "If you go along, Zander, it's a done deal."

"I think we should call up my uncle Guy and ask him," I said. "He's a policeman."

"And tell him what when he asks us about Kambui's pictures?" Bobbi asked. "If we tell him that we have a picture of Phat Tony at the mall, which just could be evidence of a felony, he *stops* being your uncle and goes back to being a cop. Are you reading me?"

"Loud and clear," I said.

"I'm sure that's what the police want to talk to me about," Kambui said. "They want me to come down to the station and look at the videos from the stickup. Man, if I do that and I see Phat Tony doing a stickup I'm going to feel stupid bad."

"You can tell them you don't know who it is," I said.

"I think I got to tell them the truth," Kambui said in this tiny little voice. "And they asked me to bring any photos I had down to the station. So Phat Tony is going to get busted for lying."

A waitress came over and took our orders. Bobbi had a grilled cheese on toast, LaShonda and I had cheeseburgers, and Kambui said he wasn't hungry. I felt sorry for him.

"And these foperoos from London contacted Scotland Yard and told them about what we were doing over here in Harlem," Bobbi said. "Let's get on a plane and go over there and beat them up!"

"Violence only leads to more violence," Kambui said.

"War is simply politics with bloodshed," LaShonda said. "And the kids at Phoenix have escalated the whole thing."

"I just brought it up as a question to them," I said. "I really blew it, right?"

"You're still the man, Zander," LaShonda said.

So what I was seeing was that we weren't wrapping our

brains around anything that smelled like a real answer and we were just venting. I knew that was all right for a while. Mom did it all the time, but it wasn't going to solve anything.

"Kambui isn't the problem," I said. "Neither are the kids from London. They're probably just looking for something to do and copped a chance to call Scotland Yard. What's making everybody on this side of the ocean miserable is whether somebody from Da Vinci did the stickup. If that did happen then Culpepper's right. It *will* mess up Da Vinci's rep.

"So let's find Phat Tony and get the deal done," I said. "Because if he didn't have anything to do with the mall bit then we can just all bust down to the police station with Kambui and fess up or whatever else they want, no sweat."

"And if Phat Tony did have something to do with it?" LaShonda asked.

"Then we stick together, because we're Cruisers," Bobbi said. "And Phat Tony has to deal on his own."

"Suppose he did have something to do with it," Kambui said, "and he's got a gun. Anybody here *habla la bang-bang?*"

"But Kambui has to go down to the police station, anyway," I said. "And the police have to do a follow-up because Scotland Yard has contacted them."

"Then the cake is done, and we just need to get it out of the oven," LaShonda said.

"Or we're done," Bobbi said.

"If we do decide to take a plane to London and beat up the kids from Phoenix, can we land the plane on Charles Lord when we get back to the States?" This from LaShonda.

"You got two votes for landing on Charles Lord," Bobbi said.

"Three!" Kambui.

"Four!" Me.

THE PALETTE

A Chance for Da Vinci to Shine
By Ellen Ravielli, Language Arts

The upcoming citywide language competition will offer an excellent forum to show off the skills of Da Vinci students. In a world that is rapidly becoming a global village, language skills are a must. In the future, one would expect every successful businessperson to speak at least two or three languages.

The competition will consist of translating a three-minute taped message and two pages of written material from either a novel or a business journal. Credit will be given for accuracy, fluency, and speed. This is a chance for our school to shine and to show it is ready to move into the realm of global affairs.

THE CRUISER

NO QUIERO GANAR NADA

By Kelly Bena

I can't help but feel that competitions are nothing more than a way to see how well one competes and have little to do with education. I don't ever remember reading that Shakespeare or Marlowe or Joyce or Toni Morrison spoke a bunch of languages. Isn't education really about depth and interest and work? I don't think the kids with the best grades are going to be tomorrow's leaders, and I don't think blue ribbons or whatever they hand out at the language competition are going to make us have a better understanding of the world. I'm not against good grades (teachers, please note!), but I don't want to be a slave to them, either.

CHAPTER TWELVE

Scotland Yard Is on the Case
as Phoenix Scholars Speed the Pace

So I'm sitting at the table eating a bowl of cereal and figuring what I'm going to say to Phat Tony when I hear somebody trying to unlock the door. Naturally, I figure it's Mom. But then the door doesn't open right away and I figure she's having trouble getting the door open because she's carrying some bundles. Maybe even Chinese food for supper.

When the door still doesn't open I think about getting up and answering it but there's no use in getting up if it's going to open any minute so I wait a bit longer. Then the door opens and it's Mom.

"Gotta pee!" she says, then scoots past me into the bathroom.

I look on the floor in the hallway and there are two shopping bags. One has those white cartons that Chinese food comes in so I pick it up. The other one has something furry in it.

"Good news! I got a health gig!" This coming through the bathroom door.

I don't like Mom talking to me when she's in the bathroom. It kind of freaks me out a little, so I don't answer.

"You hear me?" she calls out again. "I got a job in a health commercial!"

"Wait until you come out," I say. "Then tell me."

I put the bags on the table, toss what's left of my cereal (after one last mouthful) into the trash can, and sit down.

A moment later Mom comes out, wiping her hands on a paper towel. "How did your day go?" she asks.

I know she doesn't really want to know, she wants me to hear about her day.

"I killed two kids and robbed a bank," I say.

"Oh, that's sweet," she answers. "So Miriam from the yogurt company called and asked if I was interested in eating yogurt in a ten-second spot. I said yes and she asked me to come down and audition. So I go down and they have all of these really young girls and I'm thinking no way am I getting this. But they've been shooting all day and haven't come up with anyone yet so I figure I have a chance, but not a good chance. Then I figure I don't have any chance because each girl is more enthusiastic and perky than the last. So it comes to my turn and I don't feel enthusiastic and I'm never, ever perky, so I just give the script a glance and do a quick read. Like this."

Mom made me believe she was taking a spoonful of yogurt, then looking at the camera and saying, "Hey, this is pretty good!"

Then she flashes her smile, which is always her strong point.

"Then an old guy who was sitting in the corner stands up, points at me, and walks out. I had the part."

"How much?"

"Miriam is working out the details now," Mom says. "But it looks like rent for the rest of the year. Easy."

"Right on!"

"And you didn't really kill any kids, right?"

"No, but I might have to this afternoon," I say. "Remember that mall stickup I told you about?"

"Sort of," Mom answers.

"There was a mall stickup and the police picked up Phat Tony, from school," I say. "He said he wasn't at the mall, but Kambui has a picture of him at the mall on the same day as the stickup. I told some kids in London and they told Scotland Yard and they told the New York City Police Department and the police told the school and now Kambui has to go down to the police station tomorrow to answer questions."

"You think this guy — what's his name?"

"Phat Tony," I say. "I don't really think he did it but I'm going to talk to him tomorrow and ask him point-blank."

"Why?"

"Because Scotland Yard called the New York City police and they contacted the school and sort of told them that the Cruisers knew about this, and I think this is going to be Mr. Culpepper's excuse to break up the Cruisers," I say. "That, and he thinks I'm fooling around with his daughter."

"Caren?"

"Yeah."

"Are you?"

"No!"

"Zander, if you're going to fool around with girls, you should talk to your father first," Mom says. "Wait, talk to my brother, I think he knows more than your father."

"I'm not fooling around with Caren, but I'm a little nervous about talking to Phat Tony," I say. "And I don't want to talk to Uncle Guy because he's a cop. I just don't want to up and ask Phat Tony if he's guilty or not because if he tells me that he is then I might have to be a witness or something."

"When you talk to anybody with bad news, it's always good to start off with some good news, and then just sort of sneak up on it," Mom says. "And remember that maybe there are some things you don't want to know and so you have to sort of tiptoe around them. You want some stir-fried beef?"

"I think I'm going to go to cooking school over the summer," I say.

"Yes or no?"

"What kinds of things *don't* I want to know?"

"Anything you have to repeat in court," Mom says. "Would you rather have some cashew chicken?"

"Yeah, okay."

While Mom was getting the stir-fried beef I was wondering just how sneaky she was. She had all these strategies that were pretty sweet but I didn't know if I could have dealt with them if I was, like, going out with her or something. It was funny thinking about Mom as a girlfriend.

I decided to try Mom's approach. First I got Kambui, LaShonda, and Bobbi together on a conference call.

"Are you going to tell Phat Tony we're on the line?" Kambui asked.

LaShonda and Bobbi answered together, only LaShonda said yes and Bobbi said no. We agreed on no and I told them not to have their mikes open. Then I called Phat Tony.

"Hey, Zander, what's up?" he said. "You're finally calling the Godfather."

"You hear that the kids at school voted *The Cruiser* the best school newspaper?"

"Yeah, but I voted for *The Palette*, because I don't like your press agent," Phat Tony said. "She's just running your name up the pole because she's got the hots for you. It don't have anything to do with which paper is best."

"Well, we're thinking about running a story about you in the new edition," I said. "About how you claimed you weren't in the mall that day when the stickup happened and we got your picture so we know you were there."

"You don't have my picture," Phat Tony said.

"And we can prove when it was taken," I said. "So you can be charged with lying to the police."

Silence.

"So what do you have to say now?" LaShonda broke in.

"Who's on the line?" Phat Tony asked.

"If you hang up we're sending a squad car to pick you up!" Bobbi, in her lowest voice.

"Man, I didn't do anything," Phat Tony said. "I'm innocent!"

"I'll think about running the article," I said, and hung up.

Then I called the Cruisers and asked them how come they had busted the plan. They all had some kind of a lame excuse but they all seemed confident that Phat Tony was telling the truth. And we had all worked together. The Cruisers were back in business.

THE PALETTE

Is Education Optional?

By Cody Weinstein

On the PBS channel there was a show on how well an inner-city school in Detroit was doing. From what I saw the school was doing okay but not that great. What came to my mind is, Why is it newsworthy that a school has improved from doing badly to doing not so badly? Doesn't that mean that we have accepted that some parts of our population will not be well educated?

In England they are talking about allowing students to opt for a vocational track from the age of 14 on. This is at a time when nobody knows what "vocations" will even exist in 5 years. If 10,000 students choose training as carpenters, how do we know that there will be work for them in 10 years? And if there's no work, what do they do?

If I were a teacher I think that I would

advise my students to stick with an academic approach simply because it gives students more flexibility over a lifetime. Perhaps we need to look at the schools that are doing okay and the students who are just getting by and take a different approach than either sending them away from the more difficult courses into job-related tracks or pumping them up for doing just-get-by work. I don't know what to do, so don't ask me, but I do see what's going wrong.

CHAPTER THIRTEEN

I Tawt I Taw a Puddy Cat

She was looking good!

I guess, in sort of a technical kind of way, all women have breasts. I mean, my own mom has them. But I didn't expect Caren Culpepper to show up at the police station wearing makeup. Okay, back to the technical stuff. Caren is a girl and most girls can look good when they want to look good. I know that. But Caren doesn't usually have breasts that you would, like, notice. Only when she came down to the police station they were, like, you could see them!

Kambui was there, with his grandmother.

I was there, with Bobbi and LaShonda, so we had a full crew of Cruisers down at the 32nd Precinct Station House on West 135th Street. Getting Caren to come down came to me at the last moment, and I knew it was either going to work big-time or get me in a huge mess. I knew Caren would jump at the chance to get involved in anything that her father didn't like, and especially if it was with the Cruisers. I also remembered something that Benjamin Franklin said: "We must, indeed, all hang together, or most assuredly we shall all hang separately." I didn't think Mr. Culpepper would hang everybody if one of the bodies was his own daughter. I told Caren it was all hush-hush and I would understand if she couldn't make it.

"Don't tell your father," I said. Actually, I was begging.

"Don't worry about it, babe," Caren said.

Babe?

Sergeant Mike Lardner was tall, at least six feet, with red hair, blue eyes, and a kind of a crew cut that was going white around the edges. He looked like he knew a lot.

"As you all know, we had a robbery of a store at the mall a few weeks ago," Sergeant Lardner said. "Actually, we get a lot of robberies at the mall and we solve most of them pretty quickly. This week we received a message from Scotland Yard in London that told us that a school there had corresponded with Da Vinci Academy in Harlem about the stickup."

"Is this, like, one of those crimes we see on television?" Kambui's grandmother asked. "Because if this is something about running around from one country to the other I need to tell you right up front that my grandson has never left the United States of America."

"No, ma'am," Sergeant Lardner said, smiling. "This is a homespun stickup with homespun stickup guys. But as a courtesy to Scotland Yard we are doing a follow-up on their message to us, and as a courtesy to the community and to the young people at Da Vinci Academy, we have asked you down here tonight.

"What we would like you to do is to review the videotape of the crime and make any comments on it that you would like," the sergeant went on. "And if you would rather not comment, that's fine, too."

I felt my stomach tighten up twice, once when Sergeant Lardner reached for the remote to turn on the video and once when Caren reached over and put her hand on mine.

She looked like she could have been sixteen. Easy.

The video was black-and-white and grainy but we could see the inside of the shop and two customers looking at jewelry in a case. They were a young Latino couple and had a baby in a stroller. Then a young dude came in wearing a hoodie that could have been any color. He looked around, and I could see the clerk behind the counter getting fidgety. She walked over to an edge of the glass display case and I figured that was where the alarm button must have been.

The young couple walked out, the man first and then the woman pushing the stroller. I tried to imagine what they were saying.

The clerks in the store relaxed after the hoodie dude left. Then. Three guys in hoodies walked in. One looked like the same guy who had been there before. They walked quickly to the girl clerk, and one reached over the counter and pushed her along toward the cash register. The stickup was going down.

I saw one of the guys pull something from under his shirt and it looked like a gun.

"Oh, sweat!" This from Caren.

I'm looking and looking but the whole film is too grainy to really see that much.

"They're not children!" Kambui's grandmother said.

Just about then one of the guys in hoodies jumped up on a chair or maybe the counter and covered up the camera.

"He put a sock over the lens," Sergeant Lardner said. He reached over and turned off the television. "What do you think?"

"I don't think I know those guys," I said.

"Me, neither," LaShonda said.

Bobbi and Kambui were shaking their heads no and I looked at Sergeant Lardner and he seemed relaxed.

"Ma'am, what was your name again?" he asked.

"Mrs. Marie Owens." Kambui's grandmother sat up straighter.

"As Mrs. Owens said, these were not kids," Sergeant Lardner said. "They dressed in hoodies and they wore sneakers, but they weren't young people. We picked up all three of them the day after the stickup."

"You could see who they were in that video?" Bobbi asked.

"No, but good police work is not just looking at obvious clues," Sergeant Lardner said. "We began asking around, picking up a few people who were caught in the wrong place at the wrong time with either stolen goods or drugs, and we began squeezing. Eventually we got a name of one of the guys who had bragged about pulling off the holdup.

He even bragged that the police were going to think that teenagers did the crime."

"That's cold," LaShonda said.

"It is. But once we got him and he saw what kinds of time he was facing he began to cough up other names," Sergeant Lardner said. "And once we got those names we squeezed some more and solved quite a few crimes in the neighborhood. Now, this is where you guys come in."

"We didn't do anything," Caren said. "Honestly."

"I know, but you started an international investigation," Sergeant Lardner said. "Now what we need you to do is to keep quiet about this video and keep quiet about us knowing who did the stickup so we can go through the crime chain and see what else we can pick up. Can you guys do that?"

"Yeah, we can do that," Kambui said, obviously relieved.

"How about Scotland Yard?" I asked.

"We'll take care of Scotland Yard and they'll just tell the kids in London that everything is under control," Sergeant Lardner said. "That work for you?"

We all nodded, even Kambui's grandmother, but I had one more piece to get in.

"Could you tell the kids in London that the Cruisers were keeping things under control?" I asked.

"What are the Cruisers?"

"We four." Bobbi pointed to the Cruisers, one by one. "And Caren is sort of Zander's —"

"Woman," Sergeant Lardner finished Bobbi's statement. "Consider it done."

Okay, so I'm looking at Caren and she's grinning ear to ear and I'm feeling great because none of the Cruisers are in trouble and Kambui doesn't have to snitch on anybody.

I got home and Mom was making grilled mozzarella and spinach salad. It looked terrible.

It tasted worse. Maybe because it was different. I'm not a big fan of different.

"So what happened at the precinct is that we saw a videotape and we didn't recognize anybody on it," I said to Mom.

"Kambui's grandmother called me and told me," Mom said. "And that some girl came along and she's your woman."

"That's Caren Culpepper, but she's not my woman," I said.

"Then how did she get down there with your gang?"

"It's not a gang, it's the Cruisers," I said. "And she got down there because I invited her."

"So she's not in the gang, or the Cruisers, she's just your — *what?*" Mom was putting eggs in water and I was hoping she didn't add them to the cheese and spinach.

"Mom, you wouldn't understand," I said.

"Of course not, I've only been a girl all my life," Mom said. "Ask me why I'm making this dish tonight."

"Why?"

"The whole question."

"Why are you making — Mom, I don't care why you're making it."

"Because from now on I'm going to cook for you on a regular basis," she said. "No more fast food every night."

"So all we're going to have for dinner tonight is spinach and cheese and eggs?"

"You want to order something else?"

FROM THE PAGES OF *THE PALETTE*

Cruisers to the Rescue!

by CAREN CULPEPPER

Heroes! Scotland Yard has sent a letter of commendation to the New York City Police Department praising Da Vinci and especially the Cruisers for helping to keep their investigation of local crimes under wraps. Who knew that the much-maligned staff of *The Cruiser* would stand up and be counted when it most mattered? This is not Thug Life or sloppy journalism, it is international cooperation at the highest level!

And thanks to Ashley for being BIG enough to recognize it!

CHAPTER FOURTEEN

Sometimes We're Rolling, Sometimes We're Strolling, Most Times We're Just Cruising Along

Okay, so there's no girl in the world that I think can beat me. Unless maybe she's into karate or aikido or like that girl in *Kill Bill* who went around chopping everybody up. And maybe I wouldn't want to have to fight LaShonda or anybody as wild as she is. Okay, so maybe there are a lot of girls I don't want to deal with, but one girl who doesn't look very tough or fierce is Bobbi McCall, but she's sneaky. So when LaShonda decided to go up against Charles Lord by occupying his front stoop, I thought it was cute and he'd have his people just move us off his stoop and forget us. That's when Bobbi stepped in.

"Girl, we are hot right now!" she said. "We need to step to that and show Mr. Lord we are *not* playing!"

"Which is why I want the Cruisers to occupy his stoop," LaShonda said.

"If I amp it up, will you back it up?" Bobbi asked.

"All the way!" LaShonda said.

The truth was that this was getting down to a gender thing. Girls are ready to max out sometimes when the brothers (this time the brothers being me and Kambui) are ready to chill. Kambui was so relieved when he found out that Phat Tony wasn't involved in the mall stickup that all he wanted to do was back off. I was ready to chill with him. We had gotten over without getting shot or anything, we didn't have to snitch out our friends, and Caren's piece in *The Palette* had made the Cruisers look like All World Heroes.

Mr. Culpepper wasn't really happy. He was still giving me the steel eyeball when he saw me in the hallways at Da Vinci, but that was more about what I might be doing with Caren than about the mall stickup.

Bobbi was right, though. The Cruisers were on fire! So when me and LaShonda and Kambui showed up at Mr. Lord's weekly press conference in front of Abyssinian Baptist Church we were pretty confident.

Charles Lord has two bodyguards. One is a really, really black dude whose neck is as wide as his head is high. He is one funny-looking man, but you can't say anything to him because he looks like he would eat you if he could find some mustard.

The other bodyguard is a skinny little Latino guy who never learned how to smile. He is just evil-looking.

"You okay?" I asked Kambui.

"Yeah," he said. "This is all working out."

I hoped he was right, but I wasn't sure. Grown-ups have a way of making sure things don't work out.

But then *ALONG CAME BOBBI.* So what Bobbi brought along was the whole school! She had rounded up twelve kids to come occupy Mr. Lord's stoop, and the rest of the school had caught on and they all came. I loved it. There were at least fifty thousand Da Vinci kids in front of Mr. Lord's stoop. Okay, maybe fifty, but they were looking fierce!

Along came Charles Lord. He looks around and his eyes grow wide. His first bodyguard — big black dude — looks around and his eyes grow wide. Latino dude looks around and doesn't move. Everything is wonderful.

"I don't really want to deal with no children because the issues are not children's issues!" Mr. Lord's voice seemed strained.

"Suffer the little children to come unto me!" This from a woman who was just passing by.

"I am against the oppression of the poor!" Charles Lord was spitting into the microphone. "Are these elite little children — and I want to call them what they are, *children* — for the exploitation of the poor?"

"You are against the students of Harlem!" LaShonda had a handheld mike. "You have always been against us, against senior citizens, against senior workers, and now you want to attack all of us at the same time!"

That confused Charles Lord. That also confused me.

And it confused most of the people and the kids from Da Vinci Academy. But after a while I began to understand LaShonda. She was going someplace where no one knew she was going. She was in another place and, in a way, almost in another time. Away from the beaten path, away from what was expected. She was being a Cruiser on the high seas of Life.

People were looking at Charles Lord as if he was something weirder than the real Charles Lord actually was. An old woman, squat and heavy in her green dress with a scarf tied around the middle, walked up to Lord, put her double chins close to his chest, and asked him what did he have against students.

"What did they do to you?!" she asked. "And why are you against these babies?!"

Lord didn't have anything to say, but when he saw me he waved me over.

"Don't talk to him," Kambui said.

"We got him!" This from LaShonda.

I walked over to Charles Lord and looked him in the eye.

"What do you people want?" he asked.

"That you treat us as people who want to help this neighborhood," I said. "And we'll treat you the same way."

The thing with Lord is that he hadn't expected any resistance. What he thought was going to happen was that a television camera or a reporter would show up and he could spout off whatever stray thought drifted through his big head. Me and the Cruisers really didn't beat him down so much as take away his chance to spit more stupid stuff.

In the end he finally huffed a little and puffed a little, and then stormed into his house. Good. I didn't think he was going to mess with us again.

So they're holding a summer tennis camp on Saturday morning and there are two professionals in the middle of the street teaching kids how to hit a tennis ball. They're supposed to be there for an hour before moving to another part of the city. All of the Cruisers are there and we're watching from a distance because none of us know anything about tennis. The only one who is really interested is LaShonda, and she's thinking about designing something to wear that would be a really cool tennis outfit. She's doing sketches like crazy and that's pretty cool, but I'm getting ready to leave when Bobbi nudges me in the ribs.

"Hey, isn't that the kid who got kicked out of Da Vinci?" she asked.

I don't know any kid who got kicked out and I look to where she's pointing. She was talking about Syed Nolan, the boy who was being mentored and pushed Shirley down.

"Yeah, that's him," I said. "He's not interested in tennis, either."

"I wonder what he's reading," Bobbi said. "If he couldn't read at Da Vinci, what's he reading now?"

"I don't know or care," I said.

"I'm going to find out."

I was going to say don't do it, but that wasn't right because I didn't have anything against Syed, really. He just seemed like a mixed-up kid who probably needed a lot more help than we could give him.

Bobbi started over and I went with her to make sure that Syed was going to be cool with her.

What had looked like a book from down the street turned out to be some papers that Syed had folded.

"What you doing?" Bobbi asked, turning sideways so she could see the papers on the box Syed was using as a table.

"I ain't talking to you!" Syed looked from me to Bobbi, and I could see his face harden.

"That's a right triangle over a pyramid," Bobbi said, sitting next to Syed. Syed moved away about a foot, as if he didn't want Bobbi that close. "You trying to figure out the height of the pyramid?"

"No, just how tall it is," Syed said. He moved his papers away.

"I can do that!" Bobbi was getting excited. "You want me to show you?"

Nothing from Syed. He looked up at me, and I nodded. "She's good at that kind of thing," I said. "Really good."

Syed shrugged and pushed the paper to Bobbi.

"The height of the pyramid is equal to the distance from the point of measurement times the tangent of the angle leading up to the top of the pyramid," Bobbi said. "You understand that?"

"No."

"No problem, I'll show you," she said, reaching for the papers and putting them on her lap.

I stood near Bobbi and Syed for a while and I heard her explaining to him how he needed to find the distance and the angle and use a table. He asked her if she had the table and she said no, but she knew where to find one. I could see Syed getting more and more interested and the whole thing was good.

So there were the Cruisers. Kambui was taking pictures of the tennis players, LaShonda was doing her sketches, and Bobbi was teaching a kid math on the street. I felt a little left out for the moment but knew I would write something about it.

Later in the day Mom got a call from Dad. I heard him talking to her over the speakerphone.

"Most of these options are never picked up," he was saying. "So even though there's real interest in the series it'll probably never happen."

I grabbed my pen and wrote her a note: *You want to eat out tonight?*

Mom nodded yes.

Over the next few months Bobbi met with Syed once a week and tutored him in math. She said he didn't read well, but he was really good with math concepts. Maybe. Or maybe Bobbi was just so happy to find somebody to deal with in her favorite subject that she saw more in him than he had. He still seemed angry to me.

What I came away with was how much I didn't know about everything. I hadn't even heard about Fibonacci, and then I find out that his discoveries are everywhere. I didn't think my mom would get so upset about Dad getting a part in a movie, or Syed would get so upset when they tried to help him in reading. But just when I figured that out he turns out to be good in math. Go figure.

And how bright is LaShonda with her clothing and her fashions? The girl is, like, on the way to being famous, at least.

Kambui is taking pictures and putting together a portfolio

of kids around the city. We'll publish a lot of them in *The Cruiser*.

Phat Tony confused the heck out of me. He hadn't done anything wrong, but he went after the gangster role big-time. In a way the whole thing driving the last few weeks could have been the stickup at the mall, or it could have been Phat Tony wanting people to believe he was a felon. That's not cool, but I could see where he was coming from when I saw all of the rappers he had written about. What I can't see is why he would want to be somebody who gets shot up or is even capable of a felony.

Then there is Bobbi. I want to get back with her and ask her why she asked me if I thought she was gifted. If she doesn't know by now, after being tested and having everybody around her telling her, then what does that mean? And is her teaching Syed some kind of natural pattern, too?

And do I want the answers to all of these questions? Could I have partial answers, maybe just a hint or two and then I could make up my mind if I want to know the rest? That might sound stupid, but I like it.

THE CRUISER

A GRAND DESIGN

By Zander Scott

The homework that a lot of us had involved finding how many times the Fibonacci sequence either occurred in nature or was used by artists, architects, and anybody else who wanted to use the proportions that the Italian math wizard discovered. I found uses all over the place. If you check out the Internet there are lists galore and some claims that look a little wild. I can't imagine someone who built the pyramids a zillion years ago and someone in Europe or in the High Atlas Mountains all discovering the same proportions and same sequences and being fascinated by them.

I also wonder why these proportions keep cropping up in nature. It's as if there's some kind of grand design that suggests itself over and over.

Am I the only one to think it's just a little spooky?

And, oh, yes, I'm so glad that Bobbi hooked me up with Fibonacci. And I'm so glad that we're both Cruisers!

WALTER DEAN MYERS (1937–2014) was the 2012–2013 National Ambassador for Young People's Literature. He was the critically acclaimed *New York Times* bestselling author of nearly one hundred books for children and young adults. His award-winning body of work includes *Somewhere in the Darkness*, *Slam!*, and *Monster*. Mr. Myers received two Newbery Honor medals, five Coretta Scott King Author Awards, and three National Book Award Finalist citations. In addition, he was the winner of the first Michael L. Printz Award.